CAMEL
and Their
COUSINS

CONTENTS

THE CAMEL FAMILY

When people think of camels, they think of animals with one or maybe two humps.

Africa

Dromedary Camel

Asia

Bactrian Camel

2

But did you know that some members of the camel family do not have humps?

These camel cousins live in South America.

◀ *Alpacas*

▲ *Llama*

South America

▲ *Guanacos   Vicuñas* ▶

The camel has very long
eyelashes that help keep
sand out of its eyes.
It also has another eyelid
that works like the
windscreen
wiper on
a car.
This eyelid can
wipe sand out of
the camel's eye!

The camel can see through this eyelid, so, in a sandstorm, it can walk with its eyelids closed!

When the wind is blowing
the sand around, a camel
can close its nostrils
to stop the sand from
blowing up its nose!

In the hottest part of the year, a camel can go without water for about a week.

When water is available, a camel drinks huge amounts of it.

7

LLAMAS AND ALPACAS

South American camel cousins include llamas and alpacas. They don't look much like their African cousins. They are much smaller, and they don't have humps.

Llamas are used as pack animals. They are strong and sure-footed.

People shear alpacas for their beautiful soft wool.

DROMEDARY CAMELS

All camels are well suited to the places in which they live. The dromedary camel lives in the hot, sandy desert. Its big, flat feet help it walk easily in the sand.

Dromedary camels have one hump. They do not store water in this hump. They store fat in it for when food is scarce.

BACTRIAN CAMELS

Bactrian camels have two humps. This makes them easier to ride than the dromedaries.

Bactrian camels don't live in hot, flat deserts. They live in mountain deserts where it can be hot and cold.

Bactrian camels have long, shaggy wool to keep them warm.

CAMEL WORK

Camels have been used by people for thousands of years. They are able to live in places where other animals would find it hard to survive.

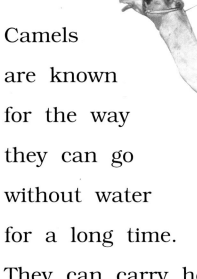

Camels
are known
for the way
they can go
without water
for a long time.
They can carry heavy loads
and walk for days under
the hot sun.

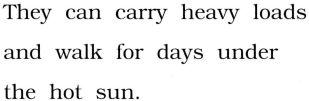

Camels are tall animals.
They have long legs. Their
owners train them to kneel
down so that they can get
on their backs or load them
with goods.

In some places, camels are used to take tourists for rides or to see the sights. In some places, camels are raced for fun.

PEOPLE AND CAMELS

Camels are important to people. People use camel wool or fur for weaving. Camels provide people with milk and meat.

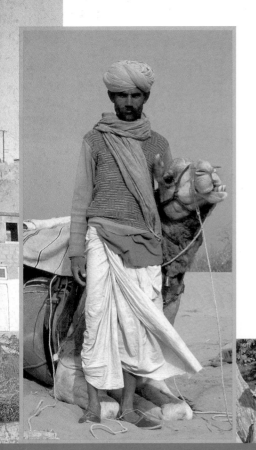

In some places, camels are used as money. When people buy something, they may pay with camels! People look after their camels well.

In the desert, most water is found in wells. Camels need people to get water for them. Camels don't like work, but they will work in return for water.

Sometimes when it rains, camels will run away from their owners. They usually come back when the rain stops.

People and camels need each other, but this doesn't mean that they always get along. Camels can have terrible tempers. If they don't like someone, they can carry a grudge for years, waiting for the perfect moment to get even with a kick or a bite.

Camels make noises when their owners pile things on their backs. They puff and grunt as they stand up. They don't really like to work. They have never learned to behave!

INDEX